D0852305

Ira Wordworthy

A Tail of Many Tales
From
the Land of Barely There

by

Stephen E. Cosgrove

Illustrated by

Wendy Edelson

DreamMaker

111 Avenida Palizada West
San Clemente, CA 92672

The Tails of Many Tales
from
The Land of Barely There

About web-enhanced SakesAlive Books

This is one of many stories from the land of Barely There. Like all stories it contains a beginning a middle and an end. Unlike other stories you have read the story continues on the internet at a site called SakesAlive™:

http://www.sakesalive.com

When you have finished reading Ira Wordworthy visit SakesAlive and continue your adventure by writing letters to the characters in this book.
If you write them they will answer you in kind with a very unique and very special e-mail from SakesAlive.

My oh my, SakesAlive
characters are living
and here they thrive.
My, oh my, SakesAlive!

sakesalive.com

Farther than far
and to the very edge
of the horizon was a path
bordered in lacy fern. If
you walked down that path
in search of lost hopes and
dreams, you would find a
land called Barely There.

Barely There… a place where wise, old owls tell stories true and laugh and laugh but never at you. Barely There… where dreams swirl and twist with clouds that fly, and the morning mist seems to sigh, "Barely There! Barely There!"

If you followed the path as it wound around Hideaway Glen, twisting through the Whisper Forest it would turn into a rutted red-clay road. Here were the fertile fields of Barely There tended by folks who care about such things.

Things were a bit more organized here; orderly rows of wheat, corn, and barley. Here chickens cluck and roosters crow as they scratch about the plants that grow.

The rutted, red-clay road wound through fields and clusters of cabins and cottages, past the old red school house with its rusty bell and stopped in the center of Tattertown, the only village in all of Barely There. It was here, too, that the only general store stood - Wordworthy's Feed, Seed and Mercantile.

Three worn, rickety steps up and you would be on the porch where barrels and wooden boxes of seeds became chairs and benches on lazy afternoons.

Early morning just after dawn the old screen door *screech-creaked* open and *crash-slammed* shut as an old gray badger stepped outside. He was always dressed the same; a starched white shirt, a black bow tie, and a crisp, clean apron tied round his chubby waist.

His name was Ira Wordworthy, the proprietor, the owner if you would, of the mercantile who swept his porch with a broom of hazel hay as the sun came up to greet the day.

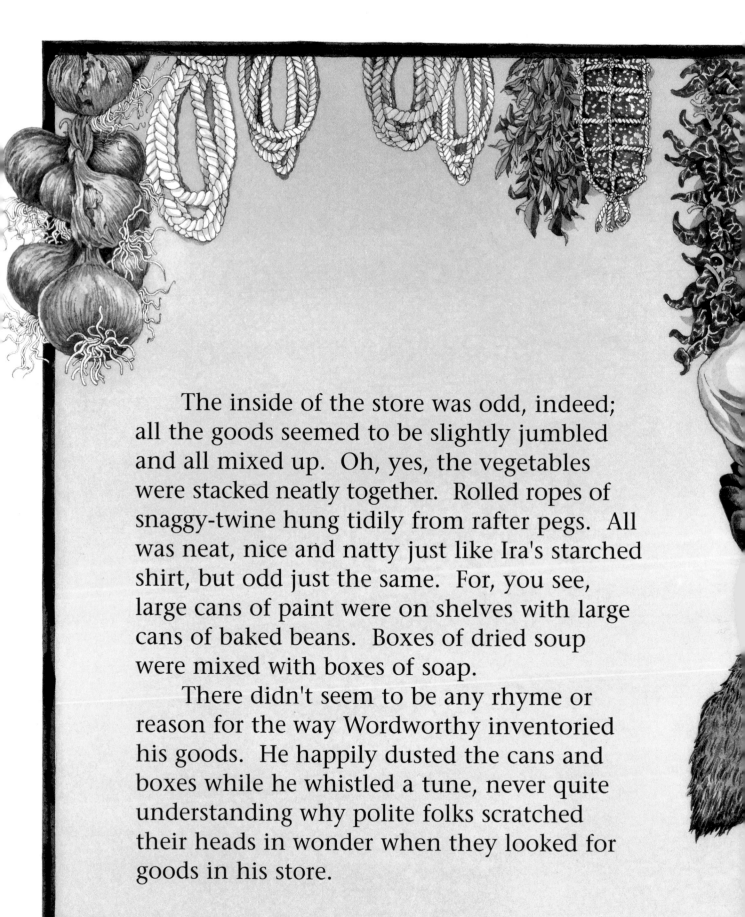

The inside of the store was odd, indeed;
all the goods seemed to be slightly jumbled
and all mixed up. Oh, yes, the vegetables
were stacked neatly together. Rolled ropes of
snaggy-twine hung tidily from rafter pegs. All
was neat, nice and natty just like Ira's starched
shirt, but odd just the same. For, you see,
large cans of paint were on shelves with large
cans of baked beans. Boxes of dried soup
were mixed with boxes of soap.

There didn't seem to be any rhyme or
reason for the way Wordworthy inventoried
his goods. He happily dusted the cans and
boxes while he whistled a tune, never quite
understanding why polite folks scratched
their heads in wonder when they looked for
goods in his store.

But Wordworthy's Feed, Seed, and
Mercantile was more than just a store; it was the
meeting place, the center of all social activity in
the land of Barely There. It was where frumpy
farmers could stand around and talk into the
wind about the weather and other wonders.

It was here, too, that the children of Barely
There came after a long day at school to buy a
soda or sarsaparilla and to giggle about those
growing up things. They would buy their
drinks and sometimes a persimmon or a plum,
and then sit on the foot-worn steps and read a
book from the library.

It was strange, but Ira didn't like the children sitting around on his steps reading. He didn't mind them drinking a pop or eating a plum, but it just plain irritated him when they pulled out their books and started to read.

"Why can't those kids just take their books and go flip those pages someplace else," he would grumble as he dusted rows of this and that. "Books and learnin' are a waste of time; those kids should be learnin' a trade or mastering the craft of farming!" he fussed and fumed.

Finally, one day he could stand no more. He threw down his feather duster and stormed into the backroom of the store where he found paint brush, and board. With a mighty flourish he painted a sign - a very important sign for things to come in the Land of Barely There.

He worked and he worked for the longest of time and finally, with a bit of paint painted on his nose and eyeglasses, he whistled in satisfaction as he stood back and looked at his handiwork.

The next afternoon, just before the end of school, Ira hung the sign on the porch outside. Oh yes, he bent a couple of nails in the process, but the sign was hung just the same.

When the school bell rang, the children, as was their wont, rushed to Wordworthy's store to buy their tasty afternoon treats.

Ira watched, arms crossed, tapping a
heavy furry foot on the porch. The children
looked at him, looked curiously at the sign,
and then dashed inside.

One by one, as Ira glared, they grabbed
and paid for their goodies. Then they zipped
back down the steps and ran off to the park to
read a bit and munch a bunch. Satisfied that
the sign had done its duty, the crotchety old
storekeeper went back inside.

The last of the children to leave the stores was a shy, little raccoon whose name was Rita. The screen door slammed as she stepped outside with an apple in her hand. She found a warm, sunny spot on the steps, and there she sat down to read, not just one book, but two!

Ira's eyes opened angrily, opened wide, as he peered at her through the window from inside. There she was, first standing, now sitting below his fresh new sign. Obviously Rita was pretending she didn't see it!

"That girl must be blind as a bat!" raged Ira as he stormed out through the screen door. He stood there tapping his foot as he loudly cleared his throat, "*Ahem*!" he muttered, "Maybe you didn't see the sign!"

"Oh, yes, Mr. Wordworthy, sir," she answered very respectively, "I saw the sign. It is very pretty."

"Pretty? Pretty, indeed!" he roared as he tapped the sign with his furry finger. "This 'pretty' sign boldly states, 'All children of the younger persuasion are not to litter or loiter or lie around reading books on these premises!' Yes, sirree, that's exactly what it says!"

Then to his surprise, little Rita looked up at the sign and quietly said, "No, it doesn't."

He stood there, grinding his teeth and knitting his brows. "Then, my furry little friend, what exactly does the sign say?"

Rita squinted her eyes and studied the sign very carefully. "Why, sir, it doesn't say a thing!"

Ira looked at the sign, studying it very carefully.
"Besides," added Rita, "why do you care if I sit on your porch and read a book?"

The little raccoon's gentle tone softened old Ira as his chin dropped to his chest, a small stingy tear trickling from his eye. "I don't want kids to read on my porch, because I guess I'm jealous," he said truthfully. "For, you see, I can't read nor write - nary a word, nary a letter."

Sure enough if you looked carefully at the sign you would see that it was nothing more than squiggles, wiggles, and smears.

Just like Rita said, it was pretty, but it said nothing at all!

Well, sir, a very good thing came out of a really bad thing.

Every night thereafter, when the store was closed at precisely half past dark, Rita sat in the flickering glow of a stubby bees wax candle and taught Ira how read and write.

As the days rolled into weeks and then months, that old badger learned the alphabet one letter at a time, and it wasn't long before he learned to read a simple storybook all by himself.

From then and thereafter Wordworthy's Feed Seed and Mercantile was a haven for the school-age children and their books. Better than best, Ira suddenly could read the writing on the boxes and cans. He had known all along that soap didn't go with soup; he just couldn't read the labels.

Oh, the *squeaking* and *slamming* of that screen door was a wondrous sound as children bustled in and out with sweets to eat and good books to read. Business was good, but Ira's mind was even better as he read book after book after book.

Minds do matter in the Land of Barely There, and books are always better when fed to eager little minds.

Everything turned out pretty well, even though old Ira never quite learned how to spell…

…in the Land of Barely There.

Now that you've read this story true, come to web and we'll share with you. There on a site called SakesAlive you'll find all the characters bright and alive. Write them a letter, one or two, and each in turn will write back to you.

My oh my, SakesAlive
characters are living
and here they thrive.
My, oh my, SakesAlive!

www.sakesalive.com